LYRA THE MEMORY THIEF

Dr. Prajnya Hegde

TANEESHA PUBLISHERS

Title   :   Lyra the Memory Thief

Author   :   Dr. Prajnya Hegde

Edition   :   First (July, 2024)

ISBN   :   9788197680809

Copyright © 2024, All Rights Reserved by Author

Published by

Regd. Add.: 254, Khuriyakhatta No. 10, Bindukhatta, Lalkuan, Nainital - 262402, Uttarakhand, India

Website : www.taneeshapublishers.in

E-mail : taneeshapublishers@gmail.com

Phone : +91 845481 2712, +91 976041 7980

Printed by :

Manipal Technologies Limited, Bengaluru - 560001, Karnataka

INDEX

Foreword

"Welcome to the world of Eridoria, a land of ancient magic, forgotten ruins, and untold wonders.

As a child, I was always fascinated by the stories my grandmother told me about this enchanted realm. Her tales of brave warriors, wise mages, and unbreakable bonds of friendship sparked my imagination and inspired me to create my own stories.

In this book, you'll follow the journey of Lyra and Renn, two young souls who embark on a quest to save their world from darkness.

Their story is one of courage, love and the power of friendship in the face of adversity.

As you read their tale, I hope you'll be reminded of the importance of these values in our own lives and the impact they can have on our world".

Preface

As I sit down to write this preface, I am filled with a sense of wonder and gratitude. Wonder at the incredible journey that Lyra and Renn have taken me on, and gratitude to the people who have supported me every step of the way.

This book is a labor of love, born from my passion for storytelling and my desire to explore the human condition. I hope that Lyra and Renn's story will inspire you, challenge you, and leave you with a sense of hope and wonder.

As you embark on this journey with me, I want to

thank those who have believed in me and my writing. Your encouragement and support means the world to me.

So let us begin this adventure together, and may the world of Eridoria come alive in your imagination!"

Acknowledgement

"I would like to extend my heartfelt gratitude to my family, for their unwavering belief in me and their patience during long writing hours.

Thank you all for helping me bring Lyra and Renn's story to the world!

I would also like to extend my heartfelt gratitude to Taneesha Publishers, for their professionalism and dedication to bringing this book to life..."

Introduction

"In the realm of Eridoria, where ancient magic whispers through the trees, a young apprentice named Lyra stumbled upon a forbidden text that would change her life forever. As she delved into the mysteries of the arcane, she uncovered a dark conspiracy that threatened to destroy the very fabric of her world.

Join Lyra on her perilous journey as she battles treacherous landscapes, formidable foes, and the shadows within herself. Will she find the courage to save Eridoria, or will the darkness consume them all?"

Lyra, a young woman of 25 with a talent for extracting memories, she had already made a name for herself in the underworld of New Eden as a master memory thief. She stood in the heart of New Eden's underworld the dimly lit club onyx pulsating with the rhythm of forgotten memories, her gaze sweeping the room with a calculating precision. Her slender fingers drummed a rhythm on the counter, a sign of her restless energy and her readiness to take on the next challenge.

Her eyes scanning the crowded room with a practiced intensity. Her raven-black hair fell in loose waves down her back, and her slender figure was clad in a black leather jacket, a signature piece that had become a part of her identity.

Her piercing green eyes with thick lashes, were a striking feature in a world where memories could be stolen. A hint at the secrets she kept, with her quick wit, sharp instincts and ability to navigate the shadows, she had built a reputation as the go-to expert for those seeking to uncover hidden secrets or erase painful memories. Lyra's appearance was a testament to her resourcefulness and adaptibility.

Her raven-black hair was often styled in a messy bob, and her piercing green eyes seemed to gleam with an inner light. She favored black leather and dark colors, which allowed her to blend into the shadows when necessary. A silver earring in the shape of a snake coiled around her left earlobe, her symbol of her ability to navigate the underworld with ease.

Lyra's past was marked by secrets and lies, her parents' memories stolen by a rival thief when she was just a teenager. She had spent years honing her skills, seeking revenge, and building a reputation as a master memory thief.

But nothing could have prepared her for the message that had arrived earlier that night: "Maya's gone. Meet me at club onyx if you want to see her again".

Lyra's heart skipped a beat as she recognised the code phrase- a warning from her missing friend.

With a deep breath, Lyra pushed aside her doubts and focused on the task at hand. She had a mission to complete, and her skills were the only thing that could get her out alive. She knew every trick in the book, but this felt personal.

Lyra's fingers danced across the memory lattice, plucking out the recollections like a master thief in the night. The air reeked of smoke and desperation, a place where secrets were currency and Lyra was the ultimate broker.

Her comms device buzzed again, a reminder of the mysterious message and the clock ticking away.

As she worked, Lyra's mind wandered to her friend Maya, whose disappearance had left a gaping hole in her life.

The message from the unknown sender had sparked a mix of emotions: concern, anger, and a hint of fear.

Lyra pushed aside her doubts and focused on the task at hand, her eyes scanning the club for potential leads.

As lyra navigated the crowded club, her black leather jacket seemed to absorb the dim light around her, making her almost invisible. Yet, her piercing green eyes shone like beacons, scanning the room with a intensity that commanded her attention.

Her raven-black hair fell in loose waves down her back, framing her heart-shaped face and accentuating her sharp jawline. The silver snake earring glinted in the faint light, a subtle hint at her profession.

As she moved through the throng of people, her slender figure weaved with a fluid grace, her long legs eating up the distance with a silent confidence. Her eyes locked onto a potential lead, and she homed in with the precision of a predator, her gaze never wavering.

"Hey, Lyra! You look like a ghost from the underworld", a voice called out from the shadows.

Lyra's eyes flashed with amusement, and she smiled, her full lips curling up. "Just keeping a low profile, Renn. You know how it is".

Renn, a fellow memory thief, nodded in understanding.

"Yeah, I do. But you're not fooling anyone with that 'invisible' act. You're still the most striking woman in the room". Lyra chuckled, her eyes sparkling with pleasure.

"That's just part of my charm, Renn. Now, what have you got for me?"

Lyra's eyes locked onto a potential lead, a shady figure lurking in the shadows. She glided through the crowd, her movements silent and calculated. As she approached the figure, her hand instinctively went to the small device on her wrist, a tool that allowed her to extract and manipulate memories.

"You're the only they call the shadow", Lyra said, her voice low and even. "I've heard you have information about Maya's disappearance".

The shadow's eyes narrowed, his gaze flicking to the device on Lyra's wrist. "I might know a thing or two. But it's going to cost you, memory thief".

Lyra and Renn's investigation led them to a seedy bar on the outskirts of New Eden, where they hoped to find a lead on Maya's disappearance. As they entered, the bartender, a gruff old man with a cybernetic eye, looked up from his drink.

"What can I get you two?" He asked, his voice dripping with skepticism.

Lyra flashed her most charming smile. "We are looking for information. A friend of ours has gone missing, and we think she might have been taken by someone who frequent this establishment".

The bartender leaned in, his voice dropping to a whisper. "They are a powerful organisation, manipulating memories for their gain. They'll stop at nothing to keep their secrets safe".

Lyra's heart raced as she realised the danger they were in. "Do you know where we can find them?"

The bartender noded. "I can give you an address, but be warned, they're heavily guarded. You'll need to be careful". As they left the bar, Lyra and Renn knew they were in over their heads. But they were determined to find Maya and uncover the truth about the shadow syndicate.

Lyra and Renn's relationship deepens as they work

together to find Maya. Lyra's past memories continue to resurface, revealing a connection to the shadow syndicate.

Renn's loyalty is tested when his own secrets are revealed. The investigation leads them to a powerful artifact that could change the course of their lives. They discover a traitor among their allies, who has been working with the shadow syndicate all along.

Lyra and Renn approached the address the bartender had given them, a towering skyscraper in the heart of New Eden's financial district. They knew they had to be careful-the shadow syndicate was rumored to have eyes and ears everywhere.

As they entered the building, they were greeted by a receptionist with a cold, calculating gaze. "Can I help you?" She asked, her voice dripping with disdain.

Lyra flashed her most confident smile. "We're here to see the ceo. We have an appointment".

The receptionist raised an eyebrow. "I wasn't aware of

any appointments. But very well, I'll check".

She gestured to a pair of heavily armed guards, who stepped forward to escort Lyra and Renn to the ceo's office. As they walked, Lyra's mind raced with possibilities. What would they find at the top of the skyscraper? And what secrets was the shadow syndicate hiding?

Lyra and Renn are captured by the shadow syndicate and must use their skills to escape. They discover a dark secret about New Eden's past and the true purpose of the shadow syndicate.

Lyra's memories continue to return, revealing a shocking connection to the ceo of the shadow syndicate.

Renn's past catches up with him, threatening to destroy their mission and their relationship. They uncover a traitor within their own organization, working secretly with the shadow syndicate.

As they entered the ceo's office, Lyra and Renn were met with a stunning vista of New Eden's skyline. But their attention was quickly focused on the ceo himself, a tall, imposing figure with eyes that seemed to bore into their souls.

"Welcome, Lyra and Renn, "he said, his voice dripping with menace. "I've been expecting you. You see, I've been playing a little game with Maya's memories. And now, it's time for the final act".

Lyra's heart raced as the ceo revealed a shocking truth: Maya was not who she seemed to be.

She was, in fact, a key player in the shadow syndicate's plans, and her memories held the key to unlocking a powerful technology that could control the very fabric of reality.

As Lyra and Renn struggled to comprehend the implications, the ceo activated a device that sent a surge of energy through the room. Lyra felt her memories begin to blur and distort, and she knew she was running out of time.

"We have to get out of here, now!" Renn yelled, grabbing Lyra's arm and pulling her towards the door. But it was too late.

The ceo's device had triggered a countdown, and the room was about to self- destruct.

"Run!" Lyra screamed, as they sprinted out of the office and into the unknown. And then everything went black.

Lyra and Renn find themselves in a desperate race against time to stop the shadow syndicate's plans. They must navigate a complex web of lies and betrayals to uncover the truth about Maya's past.

Lyra's memories continue to unravel, revealing a shocking connection to the ceo and the shadow syndicate. Renn's secrets are revealed, threatening to destroy their relationship and their mission. The countdown reaches zero, and Lyra and Renn must face the consequences of their actions.

Lyra and Renn sprinted through the streets, their footsteps echoing off the skyscrapers.

They had mere minutes to escape the shadow syndicate's agents and reach the safety of their hideout.

"We need to move faster!" Renn yelled, grabbing Lyra's hand and pulling her through a crowded market.

Lyra's heart raced as they dodged vendors and pedestrians. She could hear the agents closing in, their guns drawn. Suddenly, a black van swerved to a stop beside them. The side door slid open, revealing a dimly lit interior.

"Get in!" A voice shouted.

Lyra and Renn exchanged a glance, then leapt into the van. It sped away just as the agents reached the market, their guns blazing.

Lyra and Renn collapsed against the seats, panting. They knew they couldn't stay hidden for long. The shadow syndicate would stop at nothing to capture them.

"What's our next move?" Lyra asked, her eyes locked on Renn's. He hesitated, his expression grim. "We need to get to the underground lab. It's our only chance to uncover the truth about Maya's memories and stop the shadow syndicate once and for all".

Lyra nodded, her heart heavy with foreboding. She knew the lab was heavily guarded, and the risks were high. But she also knew they had no choice.

"As they approached the lab, Lyra's heart raced

with anticipation. She knew that the secrets hidden within it's walls could change everything. Renn's hand on her shoulder steadied her, his eyes locked on hers with a reassuring gaze. "We're in this together, Lyra' he whispered. And with that, they stepped into the unknown".

The lab was a maze of corridors and chambers, each one filled with strange equipment and eerie silence. Lyra's memories began to return, fragmented images and whispers that hinted at a dark conspiracy.

They navigated the lab with caution, avoiding security patrols and traps. Lyra's memories led them to a hidden chamber deep beneath the lab, where a single console glowed with an eerie light. "This is it, " Lyra whispered, her eyes fixed on the console. "The is where they've been hiding the truth".

Renn's eyes narrowed. "What truth?"

Lyra's fingers flew across the console, unlocking a hidden database. Images and files on the screen, revealing a shocking conspiracy.

"The shadow syndicate has been manipulating memories on a massive scale", Lyra breathed. "They've been altering history, controlling people's thoughts and actions..."

Renn's expression turned grim. "We have to stop them now."

Lyra nodded, her heart racing with determination. "We will together".

With that, they set in motion a plan to expose the shadow syndicate and free New Eden from their grasp.

The stakes were high, but Lyra and Renn ready to risk everything for the truth.

They embark on a dangerous mission to gather evidence and build a case against the shadow syndicate. They encounter unexpected allies or enemies who aid or hinder their progress. Lyra's memories continue to return, revealing more about her past and the syndicate's plans.

Renns's secrets are revealed, adding a new layer to his character and relationship with Lyra. The shadow syndicate unleashes a powerful weapon or technology to stop Lyra and Renn.

With their plan in place, Lyra and Renn set out to gather evidence and build a case against the shadow syndicate. They infiltrated high-security facilities, hacked into classified databases, and interviewed whistleblowers.

Each new discovery added another piece to the puzzle, revealing a web of corruption that went all the way to the top. But the syndicate was not about to let them expose the truth without a fight.

Agents were dispatched to capture Lyra and Renn, and they found themselves in a desperate race against time. They fought off attackers, dodged traps, and narrowly escaped capture.

As the stakes grew higher, Lyra's memories began to return with increasing clarity. She recalled her life before the syndicate, her family and friends, and the events that led her to become a memory thief. The revelations shook her to her core, but she refused to give up.

Finally, with the evidence they needed, Lyra and Renn prepared to take their findings to the authorities. But as they stood outside the government building, they were confronted by the ceo of the shadow syndicate himself.

"You fools, "he sneered. "You think you can take down

an empire? I'll crush you like insignificant rebels you are!"

Lyra smiled, a fierce determination burning within her. "We'll never back down. The truth will be revealed, and justice will be served. "

And with that, the final showdown began.

An intense battle between Lyra, Renn and the shadow syndicate's forces. A dramatic confrontation between Lyra and the ceo, with secrets revealed and emotions running high. A surprising twist that changes the course of the story and raises the stakes even higher.

A moment of truth where Lyra and Renn must decide how far they're willing to go to achieve their goal. A climatic conclusion that wraps up the story and determines the fate of New Eden.

The battle was fierce, with Lyra and Renn fighting side by side against overwhelming odds. But they refused to give up, driven by their determination to expose the truth and bring down the shadow syndicate.

Just when it seemed like all was lost, a unexpected ally appeared on the scene. Maya, the mysterious hacker, had arrived with a team of rebels, and together they turned the tide of the battle.

The ceo was captured, and Lyra confronted him with the evidence of his crimes. The truth was finally revealed to the world, and the shadow syndicate was dismantled.

But as Lyra and Renn stood victorious, they knew that their work was far from over. They had uncovered a dark conspiracy, but there were still many secrets to uncover, and many battles to fight.

And so, they continued their quest for truth and justice, armed with their skills, their courage, and their unwavering commitment to each other.

Lyra and Renn become leaders in a new movement for truth and transparency. They embark on a new mission to uncover a hidden conspiracy. They face a new enemy, more powerful and dangerous than the shadow syndicate.

They discover a shocking secret about their own pasts. They must make a difficult choice that will determine the course of their lives.

As they stood together, looking out over the city they had saved, Lyra turned to renn with a smile. "You know, I never thought I'd find someone who could keep up with me".

Lyra laughed. " I think we make a pretty good team. "

Renn's expression turned serious. "We do. and I think we're just getting started. " Lyra's heart skipped a beat as renn's eyes locked onto hers. She knew that look, that intensity. It was the look of a man who was ready to take on the world, as long as she was by his side.

And in that moment, Lyra knew that she was ready too.

Lyra and Renn share a romantic moment, solidifying their relationship. They receive a message from an unknown source, leading them to a new adventure.

They are approached by a government agent, offering them a new mission. They discover a hidden underground city, full of secrets and surprises. They are confronted by a rival memory thief, seeking to challenge their skills.

As they gazed into each other's eyes, the city around them melted away, leaving only the two of them, lost in the moment. Renn's hand reached up, brushing a strand of hair behind Lyra's ear. She felt a shiver run down her spine as his fingers grazed her skin.

"Lyra, he whispered , his voice low and husky. From the moment i met you, I knew you were different. You're the only one who understands me, who gets me".

Lyra's heart raced as Renn's eyes burned with intensity. she felt like she was drowning in their depths, but she didn't want to be saved. "Renn", she breathed, her voice barely audible. "I feel the same way. You're the only one who makes me feel alive. "

Renn's face inches from hers, his lips almost touching hers. Lyra's pulse pounded in her veins, anticipation building.

And then, in a moment that seemed to stretch into eternity, Renn's lips brushed against Lyra's, sending sparks flying through her entire body.

They deepen their kiss, losing themselves in the moment. They're interrupted by a sudden alert, pulling them back into the mission.

They're confronted by a rival agent, seeking to exploit their relationship. They uncover a hidden truth about their past, threatening to tear them apart. They embark on a new adventure, their relationship stronger than ever.

As they pulled back from the kiss, Lyra's eyes sparkled with a mix of excitement and trepidation. Renn's gaze was filled with adoration, his smile soft and gentle.

"I've wanted to do that for so long, "he whispered, his voice filled with emotion. Lyra's heart melted at his words. "I've wanted you to, " she replied, her voice barely above a whisper.

Renn's eyes crinkled at the corners as he smiled. "I'm glad we finally did. "

Lyra's smile matched his, and they shared a soft, sweet kiss, the tension between them palpable.

Just then, Maya's voice crackled through the comms device. "Lyra, Renn, we need you back at HQ. We've got a situation".

Lyra's eyes met Renn's, and they shared a nod. "on our way, " Lyra replied, her voice firm.

As they turned to leave, Renn's hand found Lyra's, their fingers intertwining like they were meant to be. They walked together, ready to face whatever lay ahead, side by side.

They return to HQ, where a new mission awaits. They're ambused by enemies, and their skills are put to the test.

They uncover a hidden plot, threatening global security. They face a personal crisis, testing their relationship. They receive a mysterious message, leading them to a new adventure.

As they entered the HQ, Lyra and Renn were greeted by Maya's serious expression. "We've received a distress signal from a nearby research facility, " she said, her eyes locked on the data screen. "Reports indicate a containment breach, and the facility is now under quarantine".

Lyra's instincts kicked in. "What kind of research were they conducting?" Maya's eyes flicked to Lyra. 'Classified, but we suspect it involves advanced biotechnology. "

Renn's grip on Lyra's hand tightened. "We need to get in there, assess the situation, and contain whatever has been unleashed. "

Lyra nodded, her mind racing with scenarios. "Let's gear up and move out. " With that, the team sprang into action, ready to face whatever dangers lay ahead.

They infiltrate the facility, navigating through treacherous labs and corridors. They encounter terrifying creatures, created by the research gone wrong. They uncover a sinister plot, involving rogue scientists and illegal experiments.

They discover a hidden underground bunker, holding secrets and surprises. They face off against a powerful villain, with a personal vendetta against Lyra and Renn.

As they navigated the treacherous facility, Lyra and Renn's skills were put to the ultimate test. They fought off hordes of creatures, avoided deadly traps, and solved complex puzzles. Finally, they reached the heart of the lab, where the source of the containment breach awaited.

In a tense showdown, they confronted the mastermind behind the sinister plot- a rogue scientist with a twisted vision for humanity's future. Lyra and Renn's determination, courage, and love for each other proved to be the decisive factors, and they emerged victorious.

With the facility secured and the threat neutralised, lyra and renn shared a moment of tender embrace, their bond stronger than ever. They knew that as long as they stood together, they could face any challenge the world threw their way. As they walked away from the facility, hand in hand, the city's skyline gleamed in the distance, symbolizing a brighter future-one that they would protect and build together.

"As Lyra and Renn gazed out at the city they had saved, they knew that their journey was far from over. With their love and determination stronger than ever, they were ready to face whatever lay ahead. And so, with a shared smile and a sense of purpose, they walked off into the sunset, ready to uncover the next mystery, face the next challenge, and write the next chapter in their epic adventure. The end. "

Epilogue

Years later, Lyra and Renn sat on a hill overlooking the rebuilt village. They watched as their children played, laughing and chasing each other through the wildflowers.

"You know, I never thought I'd find happiness again, " Lyra said, turning to Renn with a smile.

Renn's eyes crinkled at the corners. "Me neither. But here we are, living proof that even in darkness, there's always hope. "

As the sun dipped below the horizon, they knew that their story would live on, a testament to the power of courage, friendship, and the unbreakable bonds of the heart.

Author's Notes

I want to thank each and everyone of you for reading Lyra and Renn's story. It's been an incredible journey, and I'm so grateful to have shared it with all of you.

The story was inspired by my love of adventure, science of fiction, and romance. I wanted to create a strong female lead and a complex, flawed hero, and I hope I've done them justice.

Writing this story took me on a wild ride, with many late nights and cups of coffee. I learned so much about myself and my writing process, and I'm excited to apply that knowledge to future projects.

Thank you again, dear readers, for your support and enthusiasm. Keep reading and I'll keep writing!

Bibliography

- Johnson, s (2020). The history of Eridoria. New york: Random house.
- Smith, j (2019). The magic of Luminari. Journal of fantasy research, 10(2), 12-25.

www.ingramcontent.com/pod-product-compliance
Lightning Source LLC
LaVergne TN
LVHW031244190726
843493LV00010B/3003